# When They Call

L.E. Perez

ISBN-13: 978-0998102245
ISBN-10: 0998102245

Palmas Publishing 2016
www.palmaspress.com

# Acknowledgements

A very special thank you to all of the authors who participated in the second incarnation of the Thrill of the Hunt Anthology-The Hunt 2.
You have all inspired me to be a better writer and a better person.

Para Mami.

# Prologue

Her life started the day she died.

Samantha Barry always enjoyed her ride home. There was nothing better in her opinion than riding her motorcycle at night when there were fewer cars on the road.

She'd worked the late shift and the highway after midnight felt serene with just a random vehicle here or there. The sting of the wind on her face always made her smile behind her kerchief.

It was such a bright night, the moon lit up the pavement much better than the infrequent lamp posts lining the edge of the road.

She took a moment to breathe in the night air and revel in the freedom that riding her bike gave her and stole a glance at the moon.

The sound of screeching tires snapped her eyes back to the road but it was too late.

The indescribable sound of the vehicles impacting one another was immediately drowned out by the cacophony of grinding metal and breaking glass. Only the explosion of the motorcycle's gas tank managed to muffle the sound.

Sam got a final glimpse of the moon as it welcomed her to its heights before the bone breaking smash onto the concrete and the skid into the jersey wall that finally stopped her forward momentum.

She never stood a chance.

*** 

Sounds filtered in brokenly. Hushed voices.
Beep...beep...hiss.
More voices, clearer now.
Beep...beep, beep...hiss.
Children...children's cries filled her senses as they ripped through her. She could feel their fear, their pain.
Beep...beep...hiss.
What were the sounds? Who were the children?
Sam struggled to open her eyes wanting to know but the glimmer of light in the darkness faded as quickly as it came and she succumbed to its blessed peace.

***

When Sam finally opened her eyes a week after the accident she couldn't move. Pain filled her consciousness as awareness filtered in.

She stared at the ceiling panels trying to figure out where she was.
*'A hospital'*
She was in a hospital. Wait, how did she know that?
*'I told you.'*
Confused, Sam tried to move her head but was greeted with a stabbing pain radiating from the base of her skull to her forehead.

*'Stop! You need to relax'*

A tear leaked from the corner of her eye. The pain was unbearable.

The beeping sound in the room increased with every breath she took.

*'I told you, relax, you're-'*

She ignored the blinding pain and tried to move her head looking for the source of the voice.

*'Samantha'*

Panic was beginning to set in as she tried desperately to understand.

Sam tried to call out but the tube down her throat prevented it.

The beeping was faster now as the sound of children crying grew louder in her head. The children cried for her, they needed her, she needed to get to them. But who were they?

*'Just breathe, slowly, it'll be alright, I-'*

The machine shifted from a beep to a shrill alarm as Sam went into cardiac arrest, the solitary voice echoing in her head.

*-promise.'*

# Chapter 1

"Are you sure you want to do this?"

Samantha Barry grabbed her beat up leather jacket and gave her mom a peck on the cheek.

"Yes I'm sure." Shrugging into it she picked up her pack. "I won't be gone long."

Biting her lower lip, Madeline Barry watched as her daughter finished lashing her pack to the back of her motorcycle. She hated seeing her leave. Her plan to travel down to Florida on a motorcycle terrified her.

Madeline had watched her daughter die twice less than a year ago after being hit by a drunk driver. The doctors had been amazed at her recovery, calling it nothing short of miraculous.

The broken bones had healed after numerous surgeries and though the burns and road rash along one side of her body had resisted grafting, Sam wore her scars and limp with pride.

Madeline's concern was the head injury. The motorcycle helmet Sam had been wearing that night had absolutely saved her life.

Unfortunately, the headaches and visions Sam now suffered from were something she had kept from her doctors, but she couldn't hide them from her mother.

Sam finished up and shivered in the cool air before she caught her mother watching her.

*'She's worried about you.'*

She gritted her teeth at the sudden pain in her head and gave her mother a hug.

"I promise I'll be back soon. Two weeks, tops."

She carefully threw one leg over the bike and settled in. Sam took a deep breath and set about the controlling the fear that threatened to overwhelm her whenever she got on her new bike.

This one was nothing like the one she used to own. That one had been a crazy fast Ducati. This one was a comfortable cruiser, customized just for her.

Her injuries had been severe enough that her doctor had warned against riding again but she'd thrown every expectation out the window and written her own course.

Running a hand through her hair she smoothed it back before putting her helmet on. Her thick dark hair was kept at shoulder length now.

After the accident, any vanity she'd had had been tossed out along with any peace she hoped to have.

The morning was cool but it promised to warm up as the day progressed and with her ride south, she knew she would be happy about the shorter hair in the warmer states.

Pulling her gloves on she took a satisfying breath. She felt content and in control for the first time in almost a year.

Sam started up her bike and reveled in the feel of it. The low rumble was soothing, like a lullaby for her soul. She caught her mother's eye and threw her a smile.

"Love you Mom."

"I love you too. Please call when you stop and don't forget to take a break if your leg-"

"Mom...I know, I won't push." Sam didn't have a choice about stopping but she wanted to put as many miles behind her as she could.

Without another word she pulled out of the driveway and headed out to face a destiny that had tortured her for over a year. With any luck, she would find some answers too.

*\*\*\**

*'You need to pull over.'*

"I'm fine." Sam could taste the lie on her tongue. Her right leg was throbbing, from her hip all the way to her ankle and her head felt like it was about to split.

*'There's no need to hurt yourself.'*

She drove another 14 miles before she found a truck stop to pull into. She'd only been able to travel about one hundred miles.

*'You're never going to make it this way Sam.'*

She ignored the words and parked her bike. It took her a moment to maneuver the bike into the parking spot and by the time she got off she had to catch herself as her leg started to give out.

"Dammit." Reaching into her pack she pulled out the collapsible cane she kept on hand. There were adjustments she'd had to make over the past year and this one bothered her the most.

She could tolerate the cries of the children that haunted her dreams better than she could her inability to be who she was before the accident.

Standing tall, she walked as well as she could, ignoring the sympathetic stares she got. Only one person didn't stare at her, which surprised her. The little girl pulled away from her mother and took her hand.

"I'm sorry miss."

"What?" Sam looked at the little girl in confusion.

"They don't mean to hurt you. They need you." The girl's whispered voice sent a chill up her spine.

"Emily! Leave the lady alone." The frazzled woman at the counter pulled the little girl away from Sam and yanked her toward the exit. "Go on now!"

Sam looked at her hand and at the little girl who had held it.

A slight cough snapped her out of her reverie.

"Ma'am?" The hostess stood there patiently.

"Yes, I'm sorry. One please." She let herself be seated before she let herself think about what had just happened.

*'The children know.'*

Sam gritted her teeth determined not to answer.

*'Let them guide you. Let me'*

"Haven't I?"

"I'm sorry ma'am, haven't you what?" The waitress looked at her expectantly.

"Nothing I'm sorry, I'll have a cup of coffee and..." She quickly perused the menu, "a western omelet please, light on the cheese."

"Sure, anything else?"

"No thanks." Sam watched as the waitress placed the order but not before looking back at her a time or two.

Sighing she pulled out her phone and texted her mother to let her know she was all right.

Digging around in her satchel she pulled out her notebook and skimmed through the observations she'd made in the past year. The children's cries had haunted her throughout most of her recovery.

Sometimes they were just whimpers, barely heard for months at a time, but at other times the sound threatened to drive her mad.

She had tried to understand not just the children's cries but also the voice she had been hearing since she woke up after the accident. She couldn't tell if it was male or female or even if it was real or not.

Her mother knew there was more going on than she had let on but she couldn't really speak to anyone about this, not yet.

Sam couldn't stop the chuckle that escaped her. People get locked up for less.

Stretching out her leg she raised it and let it rest on her cane. It took the edge off while she looked at her notebook. Through her journaling, observations and research, she had been driven to go to Florida. And not just anywhere in Florida either, a little town called Cassadaga.

It didn't make any sense to her and much as she tried to understand what the cries meant, she couldn't. She hoped someone there would.

*'We'll figure it out when we get there'*

Squeezing her eyes tightly at the sudden pain the voice caused she took a shallow breath. That was the other problem. The voice.

*'I'm not a problem. I've always been here'*

"Yeah," she muttered. "Says you."

The slight cough made her look up and she looked sheepishly at the waitress who had once again caught her talking to herself.

"Miss?"

"Sorry." She moved her notebook so the girl could set her cup down and pour out her coffee, purposefully avoiding the odd looks she gave her. "Thank you."

Without another word she read through her notes and the information she had been able to find.

Her 'ability' as it were, was not unique. There were a lot of documented instances of people who had been clinically dead reporting hearing voices, though they were considered as being from the other side. She didn't necessarily believe in life after death and all that but there was definitely something going on that she couldn't quantify.

In another life she had been a police officer. That was before the accident. At twenty-four she was effectively retired from duty, on an extended medical leave of absence.

She hated it. Her whole life all she wanted was to be a police officer and for all of that to end so abruptly...

"Gah!"

Sam shook her head and tried to distract herself. She pulled up the web on her phone and looked up her destination again. Cassadaga, Florida or as it was otherwise known, the Spiritualist Capital of the World. If any place would have answers for her it was there.

*'Tomorrow'*

She ignored the words and smiled up at the waitress as she set her plate down.

"Thank you." She tore into her food realizing only then that she had completely forgotten to eat earlier.

By the time she got settled back on the bike almost an hour later, her leg had stopped throbbing and she felt sated. She was still a bit apprehensive about where she was headed but she needed answers. By her calculation she would be pulling into Cassadaga safely sometime-

*'Tomorrow morning'*

"Oh shut up." She muttered.

# Chapter 2

A flat tire slowed her down right outside of Savannah so by the time she pulled up outside the Cassadaga Hotel it was time to check in.

She looked like crap and felt little better. Her head felt like it was splitting inside her helmet as she yanked it off, sweat flying everywhere. Her body hadn't fared much better.

She had pushed herself and her stumble when she got off her bike reflected the level of her exhaustion.

"Whoa there." The hand that grabbed her by the elbow was dark and calloused and belonged to the middle aged man who had gotten out of his car next to her.

"Sorry." Sam shrugged off his help and grabbed the cane for support.

"Hey...just trying to help." He leaned against the driver side door and watched as she struggled with her pack.

Unbidden tears pricked at her eyes as she fought against a broken strap, her hands cramping and so slick with sweat she couldn't get a good grip.

"Do you need some help lady?"

"No."

*'Yes'*

Pain tore through her head and the added combination of heat and exhaustion overwhelmed her as she collapsed into the man who offered to help.

"Holy..." Matthew Pence caught her as she fell and swept her up in his arms. Even with leathers on she was light as a feather.

"Gabe! Gabriel!!" He rushed into the lobby and called out for the front desk manager before laying her down on the couch.

"Dammit Matt what the hell are you-" Gabriel Evers stopped cold when he stepped out of his office.

"Who is that?"

"Hell if I know?" Matt looked down at the woman who was just beginning to stir. "Reservation?"

"There's a Sam Barry coming in today but I thought that was a guy. Shit."

He waited as the young woman opened her eyes.

"Miss? Are you okay?" He kept his deep voice gentle.

Sam took a deep breath. "I think so."

She had definitely pushed herself to hard.

She found the other man and smiled at him. "Thank you."

"My pleasure little lady. You were looking a little green around the gills, I'm glad I stayed out there."

"Me too." With a tentative smile she swung her legs onto the floor and sat up. "It was a long ride."

*'Yes it was'*

"Hmmm." Gabe slapped the side of his jeans and extended a gloved hand. "I'm Gabe, Gabe Evers, and this is Matthew Pence. This is my hotel. And you are?"

"Sam," her lips quirked at his raised eyebrows, 'sorry, Samantha Barry."

"Our mysterious reservation."

"Mysterious?" Sam gratefully accepted the cup of cold water Matthew gave her and took a sip before looking back up at him.

"Mysterious. We don't usually have folks traipsing through here in the middle of August. You may not have noticed but it's hot as blazes out there." Pulling off his gloves he wiped the sweat off his forehead.

She took another sip of the cold water. "Oh, I noticed. A little too well I'm afraid. I'm sorry I showed up this way but would you mind if we continue this conversation a little later? I think some rest is in order." She moved to stand but was pushed back down.

"Let me go get your stuff first." Matthew didn't wait for her acknowledgement.

"Is he always like that?"

"No, but I think he likes you." Gabe tried not to notice the way she brushed the hair out of her eyes. She was breathtakingly pretty. He wondered about the scar on one side of her face that did nothing to detract from her beauty.

"So, what brings you to Cassadaga? Psychics, séances?"

*'I like him'*

Sam bit her lip.

"Research…I'm looking into something."

"Oh?" Gabe looked up her reservation and keyed the key card for her room. "Here you go, three nights correct?"

"Possibly more if that's okay?" She got up unsteadily and signed the paperwork he presented. She really had pushed herself. All she wanted was to take a hot bath, grab a bite to eat and get a good night's sleep.

"Here you go Miss." Grateful, Sam watched as Matthew brought in her pack and handed her the cane. "Thought you might be wanting this. Bad leg?"

"You could say that."

Sam grabbed the pack and slung it across her shoulder. "Thanks for your help."

Grabbing her cane, she turned back to Gabe. "Elevator?"

"Sorry no," He couldn't help but glance at the cane. "Listen, I can switch you to a room on the first floor."

Sam turned away. "No. No thank you."

Both men watched as she limped away and waited until they heard her footfalls on the far stairs.

Matthew let out a long whistle.

"Well...she's not from around here, that's for sure."

"Hmm." Gabe looked down at the address on her registration. "Alexandria, Virginia, wonder why she's here."

"If anyone can find out, you can Gabe."

"I don't do that anymore Matt."

"Uh huh...Oh, here." Matt pulled a crumpled letter out of his back pocket. "Miriam wants a word with you."

"She could've called." Miriam West ran the diner down the street among other things.

"You know she's old school, likes writing notes."

"Damn." Gabe glared at him as he left. Tossing the letter on the front desk he went back to his newspaper. It didn't take long before curiosity got the better of him and he pulled out Sam's information again.

"What are you doing in Cassadaga Samantha Barry?"

# Chapter 3

Sam threw herself onto the bed the minute she walked into her hotel room. What the hell was she doing here? She rolled over onto her back and groaned. The cries had started again just as she crossed into Florida and it was costing her to stay focused.

*'Sleep'*

"Stop it!" Grabbing her head, she couldn't stop the tears. The pain was unbearable of late and the temptation to abuse the pain meds she had was something she had to fight more and more.

Her hands shook as she wiped away her tears. She had driven all this way because she couldn't take it anymore. She had set up an appointment for a reading tomorrow so she could begin to figure everything out and hopefully control the voice and the cries.

Pulling her bag over she took out her toiletries and fresh clothes. The wonderful smells from the hotel restaurant were making her stomach rumble and all she wanted for the evening was to freshen up and get something to eat.

***

Gabe knocked on the door and waited. The sound of the shower running made him smile but he quickly stopped himself. Miriam's note had been more for his guest than him. Apparently, she had an appointment the next day with Miriam herself for a reading and now he had questions.

He'd done his best to tame his curiosity but it had gotten the better of him and now here he was.

Hand raised to knock again he took a step back when the door swung open.

Water dripped on the floor as a very wet and frazzled Samantha Barry answered the door.

With a nervous swallow, he watched as she fought to keep the large towel wrapped around her.

"Yes?"

It took him a moment to realize he was staring, "I... There is a message for you from Ms. Miriam about your appointment tomorrow."

Sam smiled at his stutter and tilted her head for him to continue.

"Uhm...I left the letter at the front desk." *Idiot*, he thought. He was so intent on questioning her he forgot to bring the reason he was there.

"I'll be down in about fifteen minutes."

"Sure, sure." He cursed at himself when she closed the door.

What the hell had he been thinking?

Closing his eyes, he could still see her standing there. There were more scars evident on the exposed parts of her body, but just like the one on her face they did not detract from the beauty he had just been exposed to.

The confidant way she had stared him down even as she tried to hold the towel around her had made him feel something he hadn't felt in some time. Desire.

*\*\*\**

Sam chuckled to herself as she closed the door. It had been a long time since anyone had looked at her like that. It had taken time but she wasn't ashamed of her scars and if he could look at her like that...
*'You need to stay focused'*
She ignored the familiar stab of pain and got dressed. It wasn't until she headed down that the cries started again.

*\*\*\**

"Why Cassadaga? Couldn't you see someone up north?"
Sam stopped in her tracks as Gabe blurted out the accusing question.
Ignoring him she held out her hand and waited for him to hand her the note.
"What, no answer?"
Her head was already pounding and now she was furious. Who the hell was this stranger to tell her what she needed. He hadn't lived her life for the past year.
"I'm not sure what you're talking about."
"That note in your hand is from one of the most well-known spiritualists in the country. She doesn't do readings for just anyone."
Sam ignored him as she read the note and breathed a sigh of relief. When she heard who the note was from she had feared that her trip would be for nothing.

"Well?" Gabe was on a roll and he had no idea why.

Furious Sam shook her head. "You don't understand; no one could help me. All they wanted was my money." Her voice rose with every breath. "I need the crying to stop. I need this voice in my head to stop!"

*'Breathe'*

"Shut up! God..." She collapsed against him as pain ripped through her skull. It was getting worse and unless she was able to stop it or control it somehow she knew she would not survive.

Gabe fought his instincts against self-preservation and held her tight his cheek resting against her head.

Her pain became his and as he felt her relax against him he clenched his teeth against the wave of pain he absorbed from her. It almost knocked him to his knees.

"I'm sorry." He whispered absently.

Sam felt the pain melt away and looked up at him in astonishment.

"How?" She felt practically euphoric without the pain. "How did you do that?" Her words were a whisper. For the first time since waking up after the accident Sam felt like herself again. She had no idea how he had done it but somehow he had taken on her pain.

The deep lines etched on his face eased as he released his hold on her.

"Sorry." His tone was gruff and as he took a step back from her, Sam could only stare.

Sam watched as he walked behind the counter and grabbed a bottle of water from the mini-fridge.

Without another glance at her he downed it in two swallows.

"Please." She didn't know what else to say.

"I'm one of Cassadaga's oddities, an empath and psychic."

"You're not an oddity." Swallowing thickly, she tried to process what had happened but it just confused her and made her just a bit angry.

"You understand don't you? You know what's happening to me. What did happen to me after the accident."

Her impassioned and accusatory words struck him. Coming back around the counter he took her by the hand and led her to the couch. She needed whatever answers he could give her.

"The voice, the one in your head, it's a part of you now." Before she could object he continued.

"You died didn't you?"

Sam's breath caught in her chest. How could he know that?

"Don't say it." He said. "I can see the answer in your face. It doesn't happen to everyone, but some who die and 'cross over' for lack of a better term touch something on the other side and when you come back, something is woken up. That voice you hear is you, just a different version of you, more in tune. I like to think of it as your inner or true self."

"So I'm talking to myself?" Her words dripped with sarcasm. He was so serious about what he was saying. Disbelief drove her to her feet.

"Why the pain, the headaches?" She could just feel the ache starting again.

"You're fighting it. Just let it be."

"But-"

"The crying is something different." He struggled to find the words to explain and started pacing.

"The crying, is it constant, at least since your...uhm...accident?"

*'Let him help'*

Teeth clenched she let herself hear it without fighting it. Nope, still hurt.

*'Just listen to him'*

"Sam... Samantha." Gabe was forced to shake her by the shoulder when she froze in front of him.

"What happened?"

Sam dropped onto the couch and buried her head in her hands. "This is all too crazy."

He pulled up a chair and faced her. "It may well be but you came here for a reason. I may not be in the business anymore but let me help. What have you got to lose?"

Sam felt physically and emotionally drained. The cries started affecting her physically just a few weeks ago. Whenever the cries intensified she suffered severe vertigo and nausea. Before that it was more a nuisance than anything else. Research had led her to several psychics, one of them had led her here.

"How?" She looked at him with tortured eyes. "How can you help?"

"Let me go with you." Her surprised look spurred him to continue. "The voice is a positive, whether you believe right now or not. The cries though...I'm not too sure. I've never heard of anyone experiencing both. One or the other, yeah, but both..."

"So what happens to the folks who hear the cries?" She could sense his hesitation and it sent a chill up her spine.

"They don't last a year."

# Chapter 4

Sam stared at the ceiling of her hotel room trying to process all of the information that Gabe had been able to provide.

According to him, the folks they had record of who had been afflicted with the cries had all either died under mysterious circumstances or committed suicide. The only survivor that he knew of personally was Miriam West herself. Miriam had been sixteen when she was struck by lightning and had been dead for over three minutes before she was brought back but not without something hitching a ride.

Miriam's family had tried to commit her after a failed suicide attempt shortly thereafter.

She'd never told anyone in her family what was going on and had just run away from her home in Jacksonville eventually ending up in Cassadaga.

The story according to Gabe was that she had fought whatever had hitched a ride and won.

Gabe promised to go with her to see Miriam.

Before getting her something to eat and walking her back to her room he had made a point of taking her hand again, effectively easing the pain that kept her up most nights.

She couldn't sleep though.

The analytical side of her wanted to dismiss it all as bull, but she knew. In the deep recesses of her soul she knew she was on the losing side of this battle if she didn't accept help.

*'It's about time'*

"Oh shut up." She muttered.

Rolling over she reached for her journal. She didn't know what would happen tomorrow but she knew enough to trust her instincts so she started writing.

*Dear Mom...*

\*\*\*

Gabe looked down at his hands and flexed them. He had forgotten how good it felt to help someone. Unfortunately, he had also forgotten how much it could hurt to absorb someone else's pain.

The wave of pain he had taken in from her had scared him. He never believed it was possible to be in control of so much pain and the thought that Sam had been managing it for almost a year blew his mind.

He smiled at the thought of her. She was tough and different from anyone he had met since the discovery of his powers and his move to Cassadaga.

Sam had surprised him with her openness once he had explained what he knew. And while he still couldn't quite picture her as a police officer he understood the impact of the accident on her. She was looking for answers but she was also looking for purpose, something he understood all too well.

The most astonishing thing to him had been the extent of her injuries. It shouldn't have been possible for anyone to survive an accident like that. But she had, with terrifying consequences. The fact that she had brought the cries back with her scared him. But she had an inner ally that she was only now beginning to accept.

He truly hoped Miriam would be able to help her.

Before saying goodnight he'd asked her if he could hold her hand and when she had allowed him to he had made a point of absorbing as much of her pain as he could. Her gratitude had shown on her face when they had finally parted ways.

Something about her had touched him. As an empath he was able to get a read on people but with her there was a significant difference.

There was a light in her that shone through the pain. It was a light he had heard about but never touched until now. She was special but what would happen when the cries got louder, what would happen when they called?

# Chapter 5

What should have been a good night's sleep, was anything but.

The cries haunted Sam throughout the night, mingling with whispered voices similar to when she had woken after her accident. They didn't sound very much like children anymore.

By the time she was able to drag her tired broken body out of bed it was already after nine.

*'Wakey, wakey'*

The pain that hit with those words was bearable but the sound of the cries was non-stop now playing like a bad song.

Try as she might, she couldn't drown them out and as soon as she thought that she might be feeling sick, she was, barely making it into the bathroom to get rid of what remained of last night's meal.

"Ugh..." She rinsed out her mouth and brushed her teeth. The throwing up was new. She felt more unsteady than usual. Things felt different. She felt different.

She glanced at herself in in the mirror. She still hadn't regained all of the weight she'd lost during her recovery but she hadn't lost any of her spark. Each scar on her body told the story of the accident. The road rash scars, the burn scars, the surgical scars. They were all healed. She hoped this Miriam West could heal the rest of her.

*** 

"Yo Gabe!" Matthew knocked on the front counter and went around to the closed door when he didn't get an answer.

Knocking briskly, "Gabe?" It wasn't like his friend to not be up and about.

The Gabe that answered the door was someone he barely recognized.

"Damn boy, you look like crap."

Matt's laughter echoed in Gabe's head. He felt like he had a hangover and apparently he looked like he did too.

"Shut up Matt and make me a cup of coffee." He headed back into his small apartment to change. Last night had been rough. His empathic abilities fed off him so the more he used them the more he needed to replenish himself and he hadn't. Sometime in the night he had drunk a half gallon of orange juice and he still felt awful, the vestiges of Sam's pain mixed in with his exhaustion.

Matt peppered him with questions as soon as he came back out.

"So, what's up with the mystery lady? What did Miriam have to say? Did she tell you anything about that limp of hers? Why is she here?"

Ignoring him he drank some of the coffee Matt had made. "Yuck!" Awful as usual.

"Look, we talked okay? And yes I'm going to try and help her out but anything else you'll have to find out from her."

"Aww, come on G-"

"No." He looked at his watch. "She should be down in a few, leave her alone okay?" His tone softened when he referred to her.

Matt took notice of how he referred to her and gave his friend a broad smile. Gabe liked her and that was good enough for him.

"No problem, scout's honor." Hand raised in a three finger salute he brought it down quickly when he heard the voice of the lady in question.

*** 

"Hello?" She tapped the bell on the counter and took a step back when Matt appeared instead of Gabe.

"Hey there little lady, feeling better?"

"Yes, thank you, is Gabe in?" She tried to peek around him with no success.

"He is. He's getting respectable." Matt came around the desk and offered his arm. "Shall we wait?"

Sam gave him a small laugh. The cries were intense now almost like they knew she was trying to find answers. Foregoing the cane, she relied on his arm to escort her to the couch.

They sat for just ten minutes before Gabe rushed out.

"Hey, sorry I'm late."

"You're not, I'm just anxious. I couldn't stay in the room any longer."

"Well, Miriam should be in. Your appointment isn't for another hour but I'm sure she wouldn't mind seeing you earlier."

"I was hoping you'd say that."

She clenched her teeth as she stood. The cries felt like frantic fingernails on a chalkboard now.

"You okay?" Gabe couldn't hide his concern, not giving a damn that Matt was there to witness it.

Sam shook her head. "No, it's getting worse. What if...?"

"Nope, no what ifs. Think positive remember?"

They both smiled knowingly at one another oblivious to the fact that they weren't alone.

"Well, you two run along then. I've got the hotel covered till you get back." It wasn't the first time he'd covered for Gabe but he had been surprised to get a call so late last night. Regardless, he would be here when they got back with a heck of a lot more questions.

# Chapter 6

YOU NEED TO ANSWER WHEN THEY CALL

The sign outside Miriam West's home didn't make any sense to Sam but it obviously meant something to the woman she was about to see considering its prominence in front of her home.

The brightly colored cottage was located just a few hundred feet from the diner she ran. There was all manner of talismans located on the property but what stood out the most was definitely the sign.

Gabe never got a chance to ring the doorbell before the door was whipped open. The woman who greeted them smiled knowingly before waving them in.

"Come in, come in. Hello Gabriel you're looking well."

"Hey Miriam, this Sam."

"Yes, yes, I know, Samantha Barry. Your email was a bit cryptic but the referral was sound." She pushed them both toward the flowered couch against the far wall.

"Sit, sit. I'll get us some tea and we can talk a bit."

Sam watched her leave and couldn't suppress a shiver.

*'Get out'*

"What's wrong?" Gabe saw the change in her as soon as she sat down.

*'Get out now'*

Fingers pressed against her temples Sam rocked back and forth as the pain intensified. The cries were drowning out any sound and she could only stare at him.

"Sam...?"

"We have to get out." She lurched to her feet and headed for the door on shaky legs.

Tearing the door open she walked as quickly as she could back toward the hotel. She caught some of Gabe's apology to Miriam but she didn't care. She needed to get away from there as soon as possible. She'd almost made it to the door when Gabe caught up.

"What the hell was that about?" He grabbed her roughly by the shoulders and forced him to look at him. She was white as a sheet.

He looked up and down the street and made a decision. Taking her by the elbow he steered her toward his car. Getting her settled, he jogged around to the driver's side and got in.

"Where are we going?" Her voice was laced with pain.

"Anywhere but here." Putting the car into gear, he drove. Straight out of town and down the road. He drove for ten minutes before pulling over.

When she reached over and grabbed his hand, he knew that the pain had become unbearable and he allowed her to share it with him.

It was a few minutes before either of them could speak.

"She can't help me." Sam's voice was hoarse. She didn't know what had happened, but when she stepped into that house it had all clicked.

"What do you mean, I thought-"

"We thought wrong." She didn't know how to explain what she knew. Not just what she suspected, but what she knew with absolute truth.

He had no response to that so he let her continue.

She took a deep shaky breath. The ringing cries in her head had enveloped her when she walked in that house. They were there as well and what she had finally figured out was that there was a very good reason Miriam was the only one known to survive the cries. She fed them.

When they called, she fed them. The voice in her head was exactly what Gabe had said, a gift. But even it had been fooled initially until the moment Sam had walked into that woman's house.

"She survived those cries by giving them others, people like me looking for help. That's why she's so 'well renowned' and so selective."

Gabe had to laugh. "You're crazy."

"Am I? It got worse the closer I got and when I went in there my little subconscious friend spoke to me quite clearly. It said get out. The moment I acknowledged it the cries got worse. I don't even know how to explain what I felt in there Gabe...I... I felt like I was dying."

Gabe tried to process what she was saying. It was crazy, right? There was no way it could be true, and yet...Miriam's history was shrouded in wild stories.

It was hard to know what was true or not. Add in the fact that Miriam was the one who had encouraged him not to use his abilities when they would obviously help those suffering like Sam was. Was it possible?

"You don't believe me." She said flatly. "You know what, I don't care. Take me back. I need to get the hell away from here."

His touch was already wearing off and the proximity to Cassadaga was not making her condition any better. On the contrary, she felt worse than she had ever felt, even after the accident.

*'Let him help'*

"You can't leave until you get your answers." He was trying to understand and her inner voice's warning was doing more to convince him.

*'Together, you can do it together.'*

Sam closed her eyes against the dull ache. This couldn't be real.

*'You can't let her continue to hurt people'*

"I don't care. It hurts too much." Her words were directed internally and externally.

"Dammit Sam let me help. If what you believe is true..."

Sam took a deep breath. He was right.

She couldn't let what she believed to be happening to continue.

"We need to confront her. I need to confront her but...I'm going to need your help."

Gabe knew exactly what she meant and he promised to be there every step of the way. Cassadaga was his home and he refused to let anyone take away from all the good it's done.

# Chapter 7

Gabe had given Miriam a call apologizing for their abrupt departure and had arranged for another meeting later that afternoon.

By the time they were on their way, Matt had been enlisted to help as well. He knew a lot more about Miriam's history and had told them what he knew including some of the rumors that had circulated in the past about her.

"The cries are going to be intense, you know that." Gabe was worried and scared.

"I know. I'm trusting you and that little nagging voice to keep me tethered. I'm guessing that she overcomes folks when they succumb to the cries. I'm not about to do that."

Now that she knew what she was facing, she felt better. Win or lose, the cries would end today.

*'You may lose'*

"And I may not." Gabe's puzzled look made her laugh. "Sorry, talking to myself remember?"

He shook his head; she was entirely to calm about it all.

"I'm not you know...calm that is." Sam touched his arm and smiled.

"See, I'm finally listening."

"I see that."

"It's my only advantage."

"Not your only one." He extended a hand which she took gratefully and squeezed as the cries picked up again.

"No, not my only one." She grabbed her cane and headed for the door. "We really need to talk after this if-"

"No, no ifs remember? Think positive"

\*\*\*

Miriam West lit her candles and waited. Samantha Barry had become known to her almost a year ago when the cries had started again. The cries and voices gave her no option. Samantha Barry had to give herself to them.

"You have to answer when they call, you have to answer when they call. Oh my, my, you have to answer when they call." Her singsong was familiar to anyone who visited the diner. Only she ever understood the meaning and only she ever will.

\*\*\*

Sam rang the doorbell and held her breath. She understood the sign outside Miriam's house now. She had to answer, but with what? She smiled when Gabe gave her hand a squeeze. Miriam had seemed surprised that Gabe would be accompanying her again but had taken it in stride.

The door swept open.

"Samantha my dear, are you feeling better?"

Gabe had apparently told the woman that she was on some medication that wasn't agreeing with her. She still didn't know how she felt about that but at least he had told Miriam something plausible.

"Yes, yes I am. I'm sorry about what happened earlier." Sam let herself be led in and shuddered internally when the woman took her by the hand.

"No worries dear. Why don't we have some tea and then we can do that reading you came all this way for." She stopped at the door to the kitchen. "Would you like some tea as well Gabriel?"

"Yes ma'am, thank you."

As soon as she left the room Sam let out the breath she had been holding. Being in this house was overwhelming, the cries seemed to increase exponentially. Gabe took her hand for a moment to ease her torment.

"Thank you." She whispered.

"Here we go." Miriam put the tray down and grabbed her cup. "So, are you fully recovered from your accident dear?"

Surprised at the immediate change in direction, Sam reached absently for her cup and took a sip. *'Don't'*

She immediately stopped and tried to catch Gabe's eye. He stopped before drinking anything.

Sam put her cup down and smiled at the woman sitting across from her. She ignored the bead of sweat that ran down her face.

Miriam West assessed the young woman in front of her. She had taken a sip which should be enough for her purposes but Gabriel had not. They knew. They knew about the cries. Eyes narrowed, she pasted a smile on her face.

"So, are you ready for your reading dear?"

"Actually would you mind very much if I asked you some questions?" Sam felt herself weave in her seat. There had been something in the tea.

Miriam stood up and glanced at the door. When the two locks fell in place she smiled brightly at them.

"What do you want to know?"

Sam closed her eyes as the words washed the cries over her.

"Sam... Sam!" Gabe grabbed her by the hand trying to ward off what was happening to her.

*'Open your eyes!'*

Her eyes snapped open in time to see Miriam smash her cane into the back of Gabe's head. She glared at Miriam even as the cries intensified.

"You should have come sooner dear. I might have been able to help you."

Miriam's laughter echoed in her head mixing with the cries. Sam pushed herself off from the couch and caught herself as her head spun.

"You really should have just drunk the tea dear it would have made everything so much easier."

Sam's head was spinning. When Miriam grabbed her by the hand her mind exploded. The cries became screams.

*'Fight Sam, fight!'*

"Let me go!"

Miriam's hysterical laughter echoed in her head.

She swung at the older woman and was rewarded with a palm to the chest that robbed her of breath.

"You need to answer when they call, didn't you know?"

"What do they want?" She screamed.

"They want a soul dear. They've always wanted a soul. I made a deal with them so I make sure to answer when they call. You all always find your way to me so I give them you."

Miriam pulled her over to the table covered in candles. "Ready for your reading dear?"

Sam's wobbly legs were barely holding her up and Gabe was just beginning to stir. She felt herself weakening as Miriam spoke in a language she didn't recognize and poured hot wax into Sam's palm.

*'Samantha!'*

Sam yanked her hand back and flung the candles on the table at their mistress. The tablecloth and her clothing catching fire. Miriam's screams drowned out the cries in her head. Stumbling over a fallen chair she reached Gabe and fell to her knees.

"Gabe...Gabriel..." Coughing she looked back at the spreading fire. Miriam had fallen by table and was still rolling trying to put out her clothes. Black dots marked her vision as cries called to them both. They were calling.

*'NO... Sam eyes open.'*

"I can't anymore..." Her strength was abandoning her. "I'm tired"

*'Sam! You can't give in or she wins. You can't...'*

"Sam?" Gabe groaned as he rubbed the back of his head.

Smoke...

"SAM!" He found her lying unconscious next to him. The room was full of smoke, flames across the room flared from a body by the table. Miriam.

"Dammit Sam." He couldn't tell if she was breathing. Throwing her over his shoulder in a fireman's carry he tried the front door but it locked. Without a thought he kicked at the door until it gave.

He could hear the fire truck in the distance but his focus lay in front of him.

"Dammit Sam." He started CPR when he realized she wasn't breathing.

"Don't die on me Sam, please don't die on me."

# Chapter 8

*'Samantha...Sam'*

Sam opened her eyes and looked around the room. Hospital again.

"Ugh"

"Sam?" Gabe scrambled out of the chair he had fallen asleep in.

"Water, please." Her throat felt raw. She sipped from the straw he put in her mouth and gave him a small smile. "Thanks."

"How are you feeling?"

"I don't know," she whispered. "How am I supposed to be feeling?"

"You were dosed with Rohypnol, suffered smoke inhalation and scared the crap out of me when you stopped breathing."

"Sorry, Miriam?"

"Dead...the cries?"

Sam thought about it.

*They're gone. They needed to be freed. She had corrupted them.'*

"Gone" Her tone was wistful. Her body felt like it had been through the wringer but she had survived.

"Guess I'll be going home soon."

"Yeah." Gabe patted her hand and scratched absently at the stitches on the back of his head. Things were going to be ugly for a while at home and he didn't care. All he wanted was for Sam to stay.

*'He wants you to stay.'*

Sam smiled. "I know."

"You know what?"

"Nothing, nothing...do you mind if I stay for a while? I could use a vacation."

He smiled and gave her a tender kiss.

"We both can."

# About The Author

L.E. Perez, also known as Laura E Perez, lives in Orlando, Florida and writes the stories that need to be written, be they romance, thriller, suspense, urban fantasy, or paranormal.

This is her first foray into the paranormal and who knows, she may continue the story of Sam and Gabe in another incarnation.

## Check out her website at:
www.leperez.com

## You can follow her on Facebook:

www.facebook.com/lepereznovelreads
Twitter: www.twitter.com/honorcpt
Instagram: www.instagram.com/leperezauthor
Wattpad: www.wattpad.com/lauraperez127